NETBALL GEMS

A Random House book
Published by Random House Australia Pty Ltd
Level 3, 100 Pacific Highway, North Sydney NSW 2060
www.randomhouse.com.au

Penguin
Random House
Australia

First published by Random House Australia in 2015

Random House Books is part of the Penguin Random House group of companies whose
addresses can be found at global.penguinrandomhouse.com

National Library of Australia
Cataloguing-in-Publication Entry

Creator: Gibbs, Lisa, author
Title: Chase your goal / Lisa Gibbs, Bernadette Hellard; illustrator Cat MacInnes
ISBN: 9780857987662 (pbk)
Series: Netball gems; 2
Subjects: Netball – Juvenile fiction
    Basketball – Shooting – Juvenile fiction
    Fathers and daughters – Social aspects – Juvenile fiction
Other Creators/Contributors: Hellard, Bernadette, author; MacInnes, Cat, illustrator
Dewey Number: A823.4

Cover illustration by Cat MacInnes
Cover design by Kirby Armstrong
Typeset in 15/20.7 pt Adobe Garamond by Midland Typesetters, Australia
Printed in Australia by Griffin Press, an accredited ISO AS/NZS 14001:2004 Environmental
Management System printer

Random House Australia uses papers that are natural, renewable and recyclable products and
made from wood grown in sustainable forests. The logging and manufacturing processes are
expected to conform to the environmental regulations of the country of origin.

NETBALL GEMS

Chase Your Goal

Written by
B. HELLARD and **L. GIBBS**

Illustrated by
CAT MACINNES

RANDOM HOUSE AUSTRALIA

Chapter One

Phoebe stretched up to reach an impossibly high pass. She caught it expertly and then, under pressure from the defenders, passed it on quickly. Dodging around the opposing team's Goal Defence, she raced towards the goals to catch the next pass . . . But the pass came back to her before she was ready.

Nooo!

Somehow Phoebe managed to catch it . . . But she was off balance.

Oh no! I'm going to fall!

Phoebe teetered just inside the back line of the goal circle, her heart hammering wildly in her chest. But hearing the crowd yelling encouragement strengthened her resolve and she concentrated on bending her knees to centre herself.

I can do this!

Smoothly, Phoebe turned and raised the ball above her head. The goal ring was right above her. The crowd fell silent. All eyes were on her. The Goal Defence was straining to block her view but her arms barely registered in Phoebe's vision. She pictured in her mind the ball curving over the defender's hand and through the ring. A sense of calm descended over her. She gracefully sent the ball on its arc and it sailed through the ring for another goal. The crowd went wild, yelling and stomping their feet.

With a thrill of excitement, Phoebe allowed herself a little wave to her fans before turning back to the game.

'Phoebe! Dinner's ready!' Mum called from the back door.

Phoebe dropped her arm in embarrassment. 'Okay, I'll be there in a minute, Mum.' She looked around as the crowd melted away. *One last goal before I go in.*

She grabbed the ball and bounced it off the brick wall at the side of her house. It ricocheted back, but she allowed it to bounce first on the concrete before catching it. She took one step forward and aimed for the free-standing goal ring Dad had set up for her in the backyard. The ball went up . . . up . . . and straight through for another goal.

Phoebe spent hours out here whenever she could. Her dad had created this training area for her when she'd first started NetSetGO training as a little girl and she'd been learning the basic skills and rules of netball. Practising netball was her favourite thing to do when she was at home. She loved pretending she was playing for Australia and that the crowd was cheering for her. In her fantasy, she was relaxed and confident, and everyone thought she was awesome.

Phoebe screwed up her nose. Her real life was very different to her fantasy life. *As if I could be like that in front of a crowd. I don't even feel comfortable talking to the girls in my own team!*

Her team, the Marrang Netball Club Under 13s – or the Marrang Gems, as they had named themselves – were improving their game every week, but . . .

I wish I could just relax and act normal around them!

'Phoebe!' Mum called again, sounding slightly annoyed this time.

Phoebe dropped the ball and hurried inside for dinner. Her skin was flushed and her long light-brown hair hung in a sleek plait. She could hear her dad talking in his booming voice as she approached the kitchen. Dad and Phoebe's brother Max were discussing soccer tactics, while Mum was preparing to serve up dinner. Phoebe frowned as the smell of the sarma reached her. Phoebe's mum loved to cook the traditional Croatian meal of cabbage, minced meat and rice, which she had learnt to make from her mother, but Phoebe thought it smelt horrible when it was cooking.

Phoebe slid into her seat and watched as her dad jumped out of his to demonstrate a move to Max. Dad was square and solid, but surprisingly agile.

'And then if you do this – you should be able to steal it from him.'

Dad danced around an imaginary ball, shooting his leg out at the last minute. But his foot caught the edge of his chair and he staggered across the kitchen floor, narrowly missing the hot dish Phoebe's mum was carrying to the table.

'Yeah, thanks, Dad,' Max smirked. 'I'll definitely try losing my balance and stumbling around!'

Chapter Two

Once they were all settled at the table, Phoebe's dad turned his attention to her.

'So how did training go tonight?' he asked.

'I didn't have training tonight,' Phoebe replied, confused.

'No, I meant your own training, out the back,' Dad explained.

'Oh, yeah,' Phoebe murmured. 'It was fun.' She looked down at her plate, blushing a little, hoping he hadn't seen her waving to the imaginary crowd.

'What's that?' said Dad. 'I can't hear you!'

Phoebe felt her face go even redder.

Mum put her hand on Dad's arm. She studied Phoebe for a moment. 'We all know that quiet murmur is your shy voice,' she said gently, 'but you'll need to be a bit louder. I noticed that during the warm-up at your netball game on Saturday you were talking very quietly as well. It would be a shame if the girls thought you were ignoring them. You don't want them to get the wrong idea, do you?'

'No, Mum,' said Phoebe, sighing.

Mum was right. She *had* felt extra shy at netball.

Had the girls taken me the wrong way? Phoebe thought. *Did they really think I had been rude? Is that why I haven't made friends with them as quickly as Lily and Sienna have?*

Maybe that's why Jade always looks at me as if I were an alien . . .

'How many out of ten?' asked Dad, breaking into her thoughts.

'Sorry, what, Dad?' Phoebe welcomed the change of topic but she wasn't sure what he was asking.

'Your goaling – how many can you get in out of ten?'

'I'm not sure. I wasn't counting.'

'It's really important you keep practising until you can get ten out of ten,' he said. 'Then the coach will pick you for goals every time! Why don't we go back out after dinner and see where you're at.'

Phoebe's eyes lit up. *More goaling practice before bed – cool!*

Phoebe quickly finished her dinner and headed back outside. Dad soon followed and they started with some regular goaling practice from directly in front of the goals. Dad commentated constantly as Phoebe goaled, encouraging her and admiring her technique. Still primed from her session before dinner, Phoebe managed to get nine shots in a row before one bounced back off the ring.

'Awesome work,' said Dad, passing the ball back to Phoebe. 'Now let's mix things up!'

He started Phoebe right in front of the goal ring, where she had been standing before. But this time, with each goal that went through, she had to take a step backwards, to increase the challenge, and for each one she missed she was allowed to take a step forward, to make it a little easier. Phoebe loved the new drill. She concentrated on increasing the bend in her knees to get the extra push needed for the ball to make the distance. Before long, Phoebe was shooting from beyond the distance of a standard goal circle and Dad suggested that she include sideways steps to change the angle she had to shoot at, and to increase the challenge even more. Phoebe was completely absorbed in the drill and quickly learnt to master that, too.

'You're a star!' he said. 'Where did you learn to goal so well?'

'Caitlyn,' she said. Caitlyn looked after Phoebe and Max when their parents went out. She was an amazing netballer and often came out to the backyard with Phoebe, patiently teaching her everything she knew about netball.

'Excellent. Now, let's see how you do under pressure.'

This time they repeated the drill, but Dad defended every shot. He danced around in front of her, waving his arms and pulling faces to distract her. Phoebe tried to focus on goaling but her dad looked so ridiculous that she soon started giggling.

'Dad! You can't dance around on court!'

'Doesn't matter,' he puffed. 'Just goal!'

Phoebe grinned and went back to goaling. It was hard pretending she was playing for Australia with her dad's moustache twitching every time he stretched to defend, but it was lots of fun training with him!

Chapter Three

Thick fog enveloped Phoebe on her walk to the school bus stop. Traffic sounds were muffled, the trees were still and she could barely see five metres in front of her. All was calm. Even the birds were silent. The familiar street had become a mysterious world, with shadowy shapes emerging and disappearing as she walked along. Phoebe loved it. It was like being invisible! All too often she had people bothering her, wanting to talk to her . . .

'Phoebe! Can we have a minute?'

Oh no! Not reporters again!

A chubby man emerged from the fog, hefting a camera onto his shoulder. The tall blonde woman with him thrust a large black microphone forward. Phoebe plastered a cheery smile onto her face.

'How have you managed with all the publicity lately?' said the woman. 'I mean, everyone knows who you are, especially after the camera followed you to last week's game and filmed that amazing goal you scored. The viewers love you!'

Phoebe glanced at the camera, noting the red light blinking to show it was filming. 'Oh, it's fine!' she said, casually. 'I just go about my business and pretend that no one's watching.'

'Well, we know that!' the reporter replied. 'After all, it *is* a reality show!'

Phoebe grinned, tossing her plait behind her shoulder. 'You sort of forget that the cameras are there after a while. I'm just being me!'

The reporter fired another question. 'Just between us . . .' She leant closer to Phoebe, as if sharing a secret. 'How did you get chosen to be on *Real Schoolgirls of Marrang*?'

'I was spotted in a supermarket. It was Saturday morning so I was in my netball uniform, and I was buying breakfast cereal and singing.' Phoebe laughed. 'Sometimes I just do things like that. I don't care what people think of me, I just am who I am!'

The reporter turned to the camera. 'Well, you heard it here first! Only Phoebe would have the confidence to sing in the supermarket!'

With a parting wave, Phoebe flashed a final smile at the camera. 'Make sure you watch me next week!'

Suddenly, two headlights appeared out of the fog, growing larger and clearer. As the bus pulled up to the curb, the reporters and cameras Phoebe had imagined faded away.

Turning back to reality, Phoebe climbed the steps onto the bus, banging her backpack on the door in the narrow entry. Making her way to an empty seat, she tripped on a boy's computer bag and staggered awkwardly down the aisle. The boy and his mate sniggered and the students packed into the bus all turned to stare at her.

Blushing, Phoebe slid quietly into her seat.

Chapter Four

'White line runs. Go!'

Eight girls took off. They jogged to the first white line that divided the court into three, then returned to the end of the court. Turning around, they jogged a little faster to the second white line, and again returned to the end. On the final run, they sprinted to the very end of the court, their legs flashing and their arms pumping.

'Again!'

There were eight dramatic groans, but everyone moved off in a group to repeat the drill.

Netball training for the Marrang Gems always began with some kind of warm-up. Often it was a set of simple exercises but today was particularly chilly, and Phoebe was glad that they were running.

Phoebe jogged next to Maddy and Prani. She could hear them giggling together at Prani's silly running style – she looked like a waddling duck. Phoebe wished she had a close friend in the team, someone to laugh with, the way Prani and Maddy did. She knew Charlotte pretty well but they weren't close friends or anything; they just went to the same school. She really liked Lily, though. It was Lily's mum, Janet, who was their coach. Lily was always nice to her, but Phoebe just didn't know what to do to become her friend.

After their warm-up, the girls paired off automatically, grabbing netballs for passing practice. Although this was the predictable part of each training session, and Phoebe always partnered with Charlotte, Charlotte's passes were anything but predictable! Sometimes the ball came straight to Phoebe, but other times it would go much too high or wildly off course.

'Oops! Sorry!' Charlotte apologised for the tenth time.

But Phoebe didn't mind trying to catch balls coming towards her from all over the place. It was never boring!

On the other side of the court, Phoebe heard Janet's voice.

'Sienna, you know your hair should be up. You can't practise with it blowing in your face. Go and get a hair tie out of my sports bag.'

A few moments later, Sienna sprang up from where she had been crouching near Janet's bag and walked back onto the court. 'I'm ready now,' she announced dramatically.

Each of the girls looked over at Sienna. She had one hand on her hip and she strode across the court as if she were a model on a catwalk.

The girls abandoned their passing drills and started laughing hysterically.

Sienna stopped in a theatrical pose. 'What?' she asked, innocently.

This made the other girls laugh even harder – because Sienna had used about seven hair ties to gather her hair into as many clumps, all over her head! A particularly thick clump draped down over her forehead and covered her eyes.

'I can't see very well,' Sienna added. 'Is something wrong?'

Phoebe saw that even Janet, who was busy setting up for the next drill, couldn't help but grin – Sienna just looked so funny.

Phoebe laughed along with the other girls but quickly forgot about Sienna's hair when she spotted the cones and ladders Janet was arranging on the court. There were two sets of cones running alongside each other in parallel lines, and two long, flexible ladders on the ground beside the cones.

I wonder what we have to do with those, thought Phoebe.

She looked over to the rest of her teammates to see if they were wondering the same thing. But they were now pulling out their own hair ties and rearranging their hair so that pony-tails sprang from the sides of their heads, or flopped over their faces.

Janet pressed on with the training, ignoring the girls' antics.

'Today is all about footwork and balance,' she announced. 'The cones and ladders are going to help with that. You will need to change the way you move to get around the obstacles, while keeping your body balanced. Watch my footwork as I go around the stations.'

Janet stood at the top of the ladder but side-on, so that the ladder stretched out to her right. She moved sideways along the ladder, dancing lightly on her toes, in a quick high-stepping movement between each rung.

'When you have done this several times, I'll be challenging you to look ahead, instead of down at your feet.'

Next Janet stood facing a line of cones so that the cones stretched out in front of her.

Lily moved closer to Phoebe so that she could also see what Janet was demonstrating.

'For this drill,' continued Janet, 'you need to run from the first cone to the last one. The hard part is that to get there, you will have to dodge around each cone, like this . . .' Janet took off, darting around the cones, planting her outside foot on the ground next to each one to help anchor her body and keep perfectly balanced. 'Did you watch my feet?'

Phoebe and Lily nodded, but the rest of the girls were still fiddling with their hair or laughing behind their hands at each other's crazy hairdos.

'Well then,' said Janet, 'hop into a line and let's see how you go.'

Phoebe hung back. She watched the rest of her teammates push each other forward to go first and, when they got to the front of the line, burst haphazardly into action.

It was obvious as soon as they started that they had barely listened to the instructions. Some of the girls landed awkwardly on the plastic rungs of the ladder, or wove in a curvy movement around the cones. Phoebe was sure that a few of them couldn't even see through their forward-hanging ponytails.

Most of them collapsed into giggles when they tripped.

Phoebe giggled along with the others, but she didn't feel confident enough to join in on the fun. Instead, she quietly waited for her turn and then, head down, watching where her feet needed to go, she began. It felt weird at first, to dance sideways in tiny steps. But by the time she got to the second ladder, it felt a little less awkward. The cones were a different matter. She couldn't remember how Janet's footwork had looked, so her first attempt was unbalanced and she even nudged one of the cones with her foot.

The coach's whistle blew as she turned to face the team. 'Well, that was a disaster,' she said, raising her eyebrows and looking sternly at those with the craziest hairdos. 'This time, if you make three mistakes, you'll be doing three laps of the court!'

At the threat of running laps, the girls hastily rearranged their hair so that they could see properly, and they gave their full attention when Janet demonstrated the exercise one more time.

When they tried the ladders and cones again, there was a huge improvement. On their third or fourth try, the girls were smiling in triumph as they stepped neatly between the ladder rungs and dodged around the cones. Some of them even managed to lift their eyes occasionally rather than staring intently at their feet.

'Now I'm seeing some balance!' said Janet, smiling in approval.

Chapter Five

For the last part of training, the Marrang Gems were to practise their footwork and balance in a pretend netball set-up. Janet placed each of the eight girls around the goal circle. She held only one netball.

'All of you are playing the positions of Centre and Wing Attack. As you know, when you play in these positions, you need to focus on helping your goalers. This means that when the ball is inside the goal circle, you need to stand by, ready to take a pass, in case one of the goalers needs to pass the ball out of the goal circle to get into a better position to shoot.

'Phoebe and Isabella, can you come over here? Okay. Phoebe, you're Goal Shooter and Isabella, you're Goal Keeper.'

Everyone waited expectantly, their eyes fixed on Janet.

'Phoebe will start with the ball. She has to pass the ball out of the goal circle – to any of you Wing Attacks and Centres – three times before she is allowed to shoot. Each time Phoebe passes the ball out, she will try to get into a better position to shoot for a goal. She will need to use fast footwork and focus on her balance so that she can dodge away from Isabella while she tries to get into a better position to shoot.'

All the girls nodded to show they understood what they were meant to do.

'Isabella, your job is to try to defend Phoebe. You might even manage to intercept the ball. You will need to use fast footwork and focus on your balance, as well, so that you can keep track of Phoebe everywhere she goes.

'Does anyone have any questions about how the drill works? No? Okay, great. Play!'

Phoebe passed the ball before Isabella even had time to focus. Maddy took the pass, grabbing the ball firmly, and then snapped the ball straight back to Phoebe, who had darted across the goal circle. Phoebe threw the ball back to Jade but found Isabella defending tightly against her. She dropped back and called for a lob from Jade. The high ball sailed to Phoebe, out of Isabella's reach. Phoebe took it and swung around immediately, passing the ball to Lily who was standing on the opposite side of the circle. Isabella raced over just in time to block a return pass, so Lily sent a neat bounce pass under Isabella's arm to Phoebe, who was standing by the baseline. In a matter of only seconds, Phoebe had made her three passes and had positioned herself perfectly so that she was ready to shoot! This was one drill that felt completely natural to her. It was almost exactly how she practised in her backyard! For the first time at netball training, she felt truly confident.

'Great work, Phoebe!' called Janet. 'I can see you've been practising a lot.'

Phoebe murmured her thanks shyly, looking down at the ground, but inside she was glowing.

When training finished, Phoebe walked over to where she'd put her drink bottle, at the edge of the court. Lily appeared beside her.

'You were awesome, Phoebe! I can't believe how good you were at that drill. Mum nearly swallowed her whistle!'

Phoebe smiled. What could she say back to Lily? She picked up her drink bottle, trying to think of something interesting to say and getting more and more anxious by the second that Lily would give up trying to talk to her and walk away.

'So tell me your secret,' Lily chatted on.

'Um . . .' Phoebe looked away. 'Well, I do a lot of passing and shooting practice at home.' Her voice was so quiet she could barely hear it herself.

Lily stopped walking and looked at her expectantly. 'What? I can't hear you. YOU'LL HAVE TO SPEAK LOUDER!' She grinned and gave Phoebe a nudge.

Lily's friendly teasing made Phoebe feel more relaxed, so that this time she spoke loudly. 'I do a lot of passing and shooting practice at home.'

'Do you have a goal ring in the backyard?' asked Lily.

'Yeah . . . And I also have a mini goal circle painted on the concrete, and it's set up close to the back of the house so I can throw the ball against the wall instead of someone passing it to me . . .'

'No way!' said Lily. 'That's seriously cool!'

Phoebe gave Lily a small smile. She thought so, too. In fact, everything about today was seriously cool. She had completed the drills really well, Janet had liked how she'd played, and finally she'd spoken to Lily!

Chapter Six

Lily and Phoebe reached the other girls gathered around their water bottles and sports bags. Lily stretched over Isabella to grab her bag. As she pulled it towards her, a square white envelope fell out.

'Hey, what's this?'

All the girls gathered around.

Lily opened the envelope and read what was inside. Her eyes widened in surprise.

'What does it say?' asked Maddy.

'It's a riddle, with a . . . sort of . . . puzzle piece . . . I think. It's really weird.'

'Let me see! Yeah, pass it around!' the girls called out.

But before Lily could show anyone, Sienna said, 'Lily, I got one too! But mine came in the mail!'

'I can't believe you didn't say something earlier!' said Lily.

'Well, I got here a bit late, so I didn't have a chance to,' said Sienna.

'Did you bring yours?' asked Lily.

The rest of the girls were turning their heads from Lily to Sienna, as if they were watching a tennis match. No one had any idea what they were talking about! Sienna rummaged around in her bag, fished out her white envelope, and pulled out two pieces of paper – one a large rectangle, the other a small square. They looked identical to Lily's pieces of paper.

'So? What do they say?' demanded Jade.

The two girls began reading aloud from their large rectangular piece of paper, each with a cluster of girls peering over their shoulders.

'Here is a puzzle to be solved by you,
when you are all down at the court.

Look out for a clue, or maybe two;
don't rush, give it plenty of thought!'

Lily and Sienna looked up at each other. Everyone started speaking at once.

'What does it mean?' asked Prani.

'Who is it from?' wondered Isabella.

'It mentions the netball courts. Do you think it's from Janet?' asked Charlotte.

'Nah, it's not Mum,' said Lily. 'But I reckon it's got something to do with all of us – because it talks about all of us!'

Sienna nodded. 'Yeah, and it says there are going to be more clues coming!'

'Ooh, a mystery!' said Maddy, in an awed whisper. 'My dad loves mystery shows. Maybe it's a ransom note!'

'Seriously, Maddy?' Jade scoffed. 'No one has gone missing.'

Lily decided to get everyone back on track. 'You've forgotten about the second piece of paper we got! Move over so Sienna and I can compare our weird little squares.'

Lily nudged Prani off the seat and placed her square down where everyone could see it. There were three things written on it:

You
birth
Sunda

Sienna put her square on the seat next to Lily's.

a
on
2.00 pm

All eyes stared down at the two squares of paper. At last Charlotte ventured a question. 'Um . . . Was one of you born on a Sunday? . . . At two o'clock?'

'Don't know,' Lily muttered, staring at the two squares. 'Weird . . . Really weird.'

'Maybe it's one of those creepy chain letters that say something terrible is going to happen to you if you don't forward it to five friends,' Jade suggested.

A sea of horrified faces stared back at her.

'No, it wouldn't be that,' Sienna assured everyone.

'Maybe it's about someone's birth*day*,' Lily offered.

She picked up her square of the puzzle to have a closer look, and as she did, Charlotte squeaked. 'There's something on the back. Look!'

Lily turned her square over and saw that there was a coloured splotch covering the back.

Sienna snatched up her square and turned it over. There was colour on the back of her square as well!

'I can't tell what it is,' said Sienna.

Once again, everyone stared at the squares, trying desperately to see a picture in the blurred colours.

'Well, whatever it's about,' Lily said, 'we've got a few days, at least, to think about it and see what we can come up with. That's what the rhyme said – we have to solve it at the courts, and we're here on Wednesdays for training and Saturdays for the game.' She looked around the circle, a mischievous grin on her face. 'So be ready for anything. Woooo . . .' she moaned in a spooky voice.

'Yes, we're so terrified now,' said Jade, scornfully. She tossed her hair and turned away from the group, clutching her drink bottle and jacket.

Prani rolled her eyes. They were all used to this attitude from Jade.

One by one, the girls gathered their belongings and headed towards the carpark to their waiting parents.

Lily fell into step with Phoebe.

'I reckon this is pretty exciting, don't you?' Lily asked.

Phoebe nodded.

'I wonder what your clue will be. I can't wait to find out!'

Phoebe smiled.

'It's going to be huge fun! See ya!'

Chapter Seven

'What have you got that on for?'

It was moments before their game began on Saturday, and Phoebe's dad was peppering her with questions.

'Janet wants me to be Goal Keeper today.'

'Well, that's ridiculous!' Dad scoffed, loudly enough for everyone to hear. 'You shouldn't be in defence; you're the best goaler on the team. Come on, let's fix this.'

Phoebe felt herself being swept along with

her dad, who was heading towards Janet. When he had an idea in his head, it was hard to get him to listen.

'Wait, Dad,' she said, trying to slow him down so that she could explain. 'Everyone has to try different positions. I'm sure Janet will give me a different one later in the game, or next week.'

To her relief, she saw her dad pause.

'Fair enough,' he said, nodding. 'Why didn't you say so?'

Phoebe sighed. Sometimes it wasn't easy to get a word in with her dad!

'Well, you go out there, my zlata, and be the best defender you can be!'

Phoebe loved it when her dad called her his 'zlata'. It was a Croatian endearment that meant 'golden girl'.

As Phoebe trotted into position on court, Dad began cheering. 'Okay! Let's go, Marrang

Gems! Show them what you've got!' And the game hadn't even started yet!

The umpire's whistle blew and Phoebe's dad took up prime position, midway along the sidelines. He always made a point of encouraging all of the girls, not just Phoebe. He knew each of the players' names.

'Be ready, Isabella!' he called to Isabella, who was playing Goal Defence. 'Come on!'

Phoebe looked over to Isabella who looked a little startled at Phoebe's dad's enthusiasm.

Oh no, thought Phoebe. *He's weirded her out!* Phoebe watched anxiously to see what he'd do next. *Dad, please don't say anything else!*

But just then, Phoebe saw movement out of the corner of her eye. The ball landed in her opponent's hands. She hadn't even seen it coming!

'Phoebe, concentrate!'

Phoebe jumped at the sound of her dad's voice. She ran after the Burra Goal Shooter and into the goal circle. She stepped back, ready to put her arms up to defend, but she was too late! The ball was already sailing high through the air and the goal was scored.

This is a disaster! Phoebe thought.

'Don't worry, Phoebe.' Her dad's voice came from right beside her. He had moved down the sideline with the play. 'Just remember your training. You can do this.'

Her dad was right. Phoebe knew she could play better than this. *I need to stop worrying about Dad and the rest of the team and just focus on what I need to do.* She tried to think about what Janet had taught them at training. She had told them to stand close to their player – so close that their bodies touched. This was allowed as long as the other player didn't have the ball in her hands. Janet also taught them to stand side-on to their player, so that their opponent's shoulder was near their chest.

Phoebe decided to try it. She stood right up close to her opponent's side, between her and the goal post.

Hey, this really works, thought Phoebe. *I can see my player* and *the ball as it comes towards us!*

This time, when the Burra Wing Attack tried to pass the ball to the Goal Shooter, Phoebe was able to lean forward and tap it away towards Isabella, who was poised nearby, in the goal circle. She felt a rush of excitement when Isabella grabbed the ball and threw it up the court to Prani, who was playing Centre.

Phoebe was determined to try the same move again – and she did. Several more times she was able to stop the ball coming in to the Burra Goal Shooter. Eventually her opponent realised that she had to keep moving if she was going to get the ball while Phoebe was defending her!

As the game progressed, Phoebe became more and more engrossed in the play. Her father's yells and cheers from the sideline receded into the background. She found that she was able to anticipate what the Burra Goal Shooter would do because Phoebe often tried the same moves when she was a goaler. But now that she was defending, she could see what moves worked to get away from a defender. She locked those moves away in her mind to remember for the next time she was playing Goal Shooter or Goal Attack.

I'm learning so much about being a goaler by playing in defence! thought Phoebe. *I bet Dad will be surprised when I tell him!*

Chapter Eight

'Great work, Phoebe,' said Janet, when the team came off court at half-time. 'Are you okay to stay as Goal Keeper for the second half?'

Phoebe nodded happily.

'Well look at you!' Dad exclaimed. 'Beating them in defence as well! Come over here for a minute and I'll give you a few moves you can try.'

Phoebe went to follow her dad but Janet intervened. 'Phoebe, where are you going?'

'It's okay, Janet,' said Dad. 'I'm just going to give her a few tips.'

'Thanks, Bill,' Janet responded, politely but firmly, looking him straight in the eye, 'but I'm about to speak to the team, and Phoebe is part of that team.'

Phoebe looked anxiously at her dad. He opened his mouth in surprise – but didn't seem to know what to say. Phoebe knew it was almost impossible for him not to be actively involved in coaching and cheering her. It would kill him to stand back quietly while someone else advised her. But he had always told her and Max to respect the coach and the umpire, so he nodded to Phoebe to go with Janet.

Janet turned away and called the team into a huddle to discuss tactics for the second half. Phoebe stood on the outskirts of the team circle, half-facing her dad, not wanting to let him down.

When it was time to go back on court, Phoebe glanced across at her dad and was relieved to see that he had gathered himself and was standing ready to cheer for the Marrang Gems. In fact, he had already started pacing up and down along the side-line, once again calling out encouragement to different players before the game had even started!

The whistle blew and the second half began. Again, though, Phoebe found it hard to concentrate: as soon as the quarter had started, her dad had increased his pace. Phoebe watched as he trotted and shuffled along the side of the court in pace with the play.

What is he doing? wondered Phoebe, as she watched her dad.

Then she felt a hand pat her lightly on the back and a friendly voice beside her. 'Let's go, Phoebe.'

It was Lily. Phoebe smiled at her gratefully. She took a deep breath and turned back to the game. As the ball came down the court, she focused on trying to stop the Burra Goal Shooter from getting it. It still felt strange to follow her player instead of trying to get away from her, but Phoebe was determined to play as best she could. She worked hard to use her skills to catch rebounds from the goal ring throughout the third and fourth quarters.

In the final minutes of the game, the Burra Goal Shooter attempted a goal, but the ball bounced high off the ring.

This one's mine!

The Burra goalers had jumped too early, and they dropped away as Phoebe swung around, leapt up and snatched the ball out of the air. She fed it out to Lily in Wing Defence, who wasted no time passing it down to Maddy as Centre, who threw it to Sienna in Wing

Attack. Sienna passed it on, and it landed safely with Jade, the Goal Shooter, who converted it into a goal.

Lily spun around and high-fived Phoebe in delight. 'Great rebound, Phoebs!'

Phoebe tried to act cool and grin back, but her eyes were shining. Lily had called her 'Phoebs'. No one had ever given her a nickname before.

Just as the teams were positioning themselves for the next centre pass, the final whistle blew. The Gems had won! Phoebe joined her teammates in cheering, but they also remembered to shake hands with the Burra players.

'Good game.'

'Well played.'

Lily whispered in Phoebe's ear as they walked off the court. 'Isabella and Jade got an envelope each. Two more clues! Can you stay around for a little while so we can all look at them?'

Phoebe nodded – but then her dad appeared in front of her. 'How about all of those intercepts!' He wrapped her in a big bear hug. 'Now, off to the soccer to see some of Max's magic!'

Chapter Nine

Oh, no! I forgot about Max's game! How can I explain that I don't want to go?

Phoebe really didn't want to go over the whole story about the mystery puzzle. It was important to her because it felt like it was the one thing that tied her to her teammates. But if she took the time to explain all that to her dad, she might miss the whole thing!

'Um . . . Dad, I want to stay around the club for a while,' she said.

Her dad's expression changed from smiling to frowning instantly. 'You don't want to come to support your brother, even though he comes to support you?'

'It's not that,' Phoebe hastened to reassure him. 'I wanted to watch one of the senior games to . . . um . . . to see if I can pick up any skills. I can walk home later,' she added hopefully.

Dad nodded in agreement. 'Okay, my zlata, but make sure you don't get home too late.' He kissed her gently on the head, turned and headed for his car.

Phoebe watched for a moment, feeling a little guilty about not telling her dad the whole story, but then, when the coast was clear, she spun on her heel and raced towards the clubrooms, where the rest of the team was heading. She felt a zing of excitement at the idea of a mystery to solve.

Inside the clubrooms, all the girls clustered around a table against one of the windows.

Lily pulled a crumpled square of paper out of a pocket in her tracksuit pants and put it on the table. Sienna placed her square there, too.

'Before we see the next clues, maybe we should read the riddle again, just to be sure we didn't miss anything,' Lily suggested.

Jade read it aloud.

'Here is a puzzle to be solved by you,
when you are all down at the court.
Look out for a clue, or maybe two;
don't rush, give it plenty of thought!'

As soon as she finished reading, Jade placed her square on the table. It had lots of letters, but none of them made any sense!

| ed to |
| arty |
| ugust at |

Everyone stared at this new clue, their eyes travelling from one square to the other.

'Quick, Isabella, add your clue!' Maddy said.

Isabella carefully placed her clue next to the others.

arrang. e celebrity. over.

There was a burst of excited babble. A celebrity was involved!

Maddy began to shuffle the squares around, trying to match them up so that they made sense. Charlotte helped her, shifting the four squares around to see which combination worked. The rest of the team looked on, offering suggestions, which made their puzzle-solving even slower!

After a few tries, Jade yelled, 'Stop there! That's it! Look!'

You	ed to	a	arrang.
Birth	arty	on	e celebrity.
Sunda	ugust at	2.00 pm	over.

Prani jumped up and down on the spot. 'Yay! A birthday party! With a celebrity!' Wide-eyed, she breathed, 'Imagine if someone famous was there . . . Ooh, even better – imagine if it was a famous person's party!'

Jade cut her off with a wave of her hand. 'Come off it, Prani. As if the whole team would be invited to a famous person's party.' She smirked. 'Especially since *I'm* the only one here who actually knows a celebrity.'

Phoebe mentally rolled her eyes. They had all heard before about Jade's cousin who had been on *Big Brother*. But she looked down at the four clues, again. It *did* seem to be about a birthday party – and it *did* say 'celebrity'.

We just need more clues, she decided. *Hmm . . . More clues . . .*

'There might be more clues if we turn the cards over,' spoke Phoebe, quietly. 'Maybe there's some colour on the back of the new squares.'

Several of the girls were talking at once, so most of them didn't hear Phoebe. But Maddy, who was standing next to Phoebe, did. With a much louder voice, she called out, 'Turn the cards over!'

Phoebe was right. The new clues *did* have colour on the back! A new urgency fell on the girls, and they all leant in closer to examine the other side of each square.

'Oh my God,' Isabella exclaimed, waving both hands at the cards. 'Can anyone else see that? I reckon it's a photo – look! That bit is hair, and that bit could be part of a nose . . . or maybe an ear.'

Maddy and Lily tilted their heads and squinted.

'Or maybe a chin,' said Maddy.

'It's definitely a photo, though,' added Lily.

Finally they agreed to rack their brains over the next few days to see if they could crack the message. Lily, Sienna, Jade and Isabella each took back their clues, but as they all wandered out to watch the Under 17s play, they couldn't help but continue to speculate about the team mystery.

Chapter Ten

At the beginning of training the following Wednesday, Phoebe took off her jacket and put it on the bench near her water bottle. She was just retying her ponytail when she saw Maddy run up to join the group.

'I got a clue! I got a clue!'

Charlotte bounded over. 'Me too!'

'Really? Awesome!'

'Give us a look!'

'Nah, we should wait until everyone's here, otherwise Sienna will miss out.'

'I've been thinking about this and I reckon . . .'

'Where did I put it? . . .'

Everyone was talking at once. The excitement was contagious. Prani and Isabella started dancing on the spot, and Lily and Maddy chanted over and over, 'Let's do it now! Let's do it now!'

Phoebe stood nearby, staring at a pebble on the ground in front of her. *What if I don't get a clue? What if whoever's sending the mystery clues doesn't like me?* She took a deep breath, trying to shrug off the thought.

'Okay, girls,' called Janet, once Sienna had arrived. 'Come over here so we can start.'

But everyone was so caught up in the clues that no one heard!

'Girls!' Janet shouted. This time she had a

very serious expression on her face. 'Right. Listen carefully because I do not want to have to repeat this. Obviously there's something exciting going on, but you all know that while we are training or playing a match, you need to listen to me and pay attention. Do you understand?' She glared at the girls.

Phoebe swallowed nervously. She distinctly heard a loud gulp from Prani.

Janet grinned suddenly. 'But make sure you tell me what it is when the mystery's solved!'

The girls' eyes lit up. Even Janet wanted to know what the mystery was!

Janet then sent the whole team for a warm-up lap of the football ground that was next to the netball courts. It began as a subdued jog for the first hundred metres, but Sienna bounced back quickly from being told off. She took something out of her pocket with a flourish. To everyone's delight, she pulled on a pair of huge red sunglasses. At each corner of the glasses, there was a green plastic parrot perched high, poking into her hair.

She playfully jiggled them up and down on her nose. When she spoke, she drew out each word slowly for effect. 'I *reeeally* need these today, because this way, I can check out those boys over there at footy training!'

At that, all eyes turned towards the large group of boys kicking footballs in a complicated drill that covered the entire stretch of grass.

Phoebe turned back to watch Sienna, and chuckled when she saw that Sienna was now somehow wearing the glasses upside down.

They jogged slowly. All of the girls were more interested in Sienna's glasses and the boys at training than in focusing on their warm-up.

Suddenly, one of the red footballs the boys were kicking around rolled under the fence, right in front of Phoebe. Phoebe stopped to pick it up, then passed it from one hand to the other, looking to see who had kicked it out.

'Here! Kick it to me!' one of the boys called from the goal posts.

Phoebe smiled and kicked the ball over the fence to the blond-haired boy who had his arms raised.

'Thanks, Phoebe! See you at the fete!' he called. He waved at her and then turned away, kicking the ball towards one of the other boys.

Phoebe turned to start jogging again, but quickly noticed that every girl in her team had stopped and was staring at the boy. Then, one by one, their focus shifted until all of them were staring at Phoebe. She looked back, puzzled by the sudden silence. It didn't last long.

'Who's *he*?'

'What's his *name*?'

'How do you *know* him?'

'Do you know any of the *others*?'

Phoebe started walking, surrounded by her teammates, who were peppering her with questions.

'That's just Jordan,' she replied, shrugging a shoulder. She was a bit stunned to be at the centre of attention. 'He's my brother's friend. He comes over to our house all the time.'

'Oh, you lucky thing!' Jade said, sighing.

'He's *sooo* cute!' said Sienna.

'Do you like him?' asked Prani.

Phoebe shrugged both shoulders this time. 'Sure. He's nice.'

Prani giggled. 'No, we mean, do you *like* like him?'

Phoebe blushed. She answered 'Not really' – but was so quiet that no one actually heard her answer. They started to tease her.

'You *looove* him!'

'You want to *kiiiss* him!'

'You want to *maaarry* him!'

Prani made loud kissing noises in Pheobe's right ear, then Lily wrapped her arms around her, forcing her to stop walking. 'Oh Jordan, I love you *sooo* much!' she said, in a squeaky-high extra-girly voice.

Phoebe grinned, shoving Lily away. She glanced over her shoulder to check that Jordan was out of hearing range. If he heard them, she would absolutely die from embarrassment. Every time he came over to see her brother, she'd have to hide in her bedroom. Luckily he was too far away to have heard.

Phoebe turned back around, relieved. 'Well, if you're going to the fete, you can see him there,' she said.

'In that case, I'm going to be at the fete all day!' said Jade.

Phoebe smiled and took in what was happening.

For the very first time – finally! – she was really in the middle of this group.

Not on the side looking in.

Not feeling too shy.

In the middle.

The only thing was that all the girls were so wrapped up in their conversation that they hadn't noticed Janet approaching from behind! One by one, they spotted her frowning behind Phoebe, and their faces sobered up, guiltily.

Lily, unaware, continued to squeal at Phoebe. 'But I *caaan't* live without you!'

'Well,' said Janet, 'if you get moving on the warm-up, you *won't* have to live without her!'

Lily screwed her face up when she heard her mother's tone. She gave her a small wave, then turned to start jogging, muttering to everyone. 'Just run. Trust me. Don't say another word!'

Chapter Eleven

During the passing drills, the usually loud chatter was absent. The girls felt guilty about not doing the warm-up run properly and wanted to show Janet that they were not going to muck around anymore. Each girl concentrated on passing the ball straight to her partner.

Janet nodded approvingly when she called them to gather together again. 'Today we are going to be doing a drill so that you can practise leading out for a centre pass. "Leading out" means that when the whistle blows, you move in front of your opponent so that you're free to take the centre pass. For our practice, I want you to line up behind the transverse line in pairs.'

No one moved. The whole team had blank looks on their faces. Janet raised her eyebrows at the group.

Phoebe was too shy to ask Janet what she meant. She knew that Janet had explained this a few weeks ago, and that she should remember what the transverse lines were.

'Um . . . Mum . . . Which one is the trans-whatever line, again?'

Phoebe was relieved that Lily had spoken up.

'Oh, sorry,' Janet replied. 'I should have realised you might not remember.' She smiled at the group of girls. 'The transverse lines are the lines that divide the court into thirds,' she explained, 'which means that there are two of them.' She pointed to the nearest one. 'That's the transverse line I'd like you to line up behind.'

Understanding dawned on the faces of all the girls. They headed to where Janet pointed.

'Okay, now decide with your partner who will be the attacker and who will be the defender.'

While each pair decided this, Janet grabbed a netball. She stood in the centre circle.

'When I call "play", the attacker will run forward in a straight line to try to catch the ball I pass you. Defenders, you stick with your partner. You might even manage to intercept a pass.'

Phoebe and Charlotte were the first to try. When Janet called 'play', Charlotte, who was attacking, attempted to run in a straight line towards Janet. Phoebe ran with her. When

Janet passed the ball, Phoebe stretched her arm in front of Charlotte and tapped the ball away so that Charlotte couldn't grab it.

'Good try, Charlotte. Nice work, Phoebe. Okay, next.'

Once each pair had a turn, the partners swapped roles. Phoebe began to notice that some attackers attempted different strategies to break free.

'Okay. We'll stop there,' said Janet. 'I noticed that we started with a straight lead, which was good. That's what I wanted. But when that didn't work, what did you do instead?'

'I tried to change direction.'

'I dodged a bit.'

'I ran out wider.'

'Exactly,' said Janet. 'Even though I wanted you to practise a straight lead, I was impressed that you tried other things when that tactic didn't work. Well done, everyone.' Janet paused for a moment and glanced at Jade. 'What did you try, Jade?'

'I dropped back for a lob pass,' Jade replied, confident as always.

'Yes. Does anyone know why that might not always be a good idea?'

Jade's superior smirk faded when she realised that she may have done something wrong, but Janet noticed and hastened to reassure her. 'It *can* be a very good move sometimes, Jade.'

Isabella raised her hand to answer Janet's question. 'Um . . . You could have a tall player on you, and she could jump and get the pass?'

'That's exactly right.'

For the rest of the practice session, all the girls tried extra hard with everything Janet asked them to do. They didn't dare talk about the mystery. But Phoebe couldn't help sneakily checking her watch. She could hardly wait

for training to finish so they could see what
Maddy and Charlotte's clues were.

There was just one thing still bothering her,
and it had niggled at her mind all throughout the training session. So far, six of the
girls had been sent clues. Phoebe and Prani
were the only ones on the team who hadn't
received one.

*What if it ends up that I'm the only one who
doesn't get a clue?*

Chapter Twelve

When training had finished, every one of the girls headed to the clubrooms. Usually they mucked around, shooting goals, until one by one they headed home. Lily and Janet were always the last to leave. This week, however, with hasty excuses of a 'team meeting', they had about ten minutes to see if they could solve the riddle with the help of the latest two mystery clues.

Charlotte and Maddy didn't waste any time putting their clues down on the table next to the four they already had. Lily muttered loudly enough for everyone to hear, as she puzzled over the words.

Maddy's clue read:

```
        at
      Dress
      Whose
```

Charlotte's square revealed whole words as well:

```
        M
     favourit
     Flip me
```

'Flip me?' Prani giggled. 'Maybe we have to do gymnastics for a celebrity!' She bent backwards until her hands reached the ground behind her and flipped her legs over one at a time. She righted herself and flung her arms above her head. 'Tada!'

Maddy jumped in to have a go as well, but her backwards flip was much less successful than Prani's. She ended up sprawled in the corner, laughing.

'Don't forget the finish!' Prani reminded her.

Maddy sprang up. 'Tada!' they yelled in unison, their arms flung wide.

Completely ignoring them, Lily kept muttering to herself, trying to work out where the two new clues should fit in with the others.

'Well, now it's starting to make a bit of sense,' said Jade.

You	ed to	a
birth	arty	on
Sunda	ugust at	2.00 pm

at	M	arrang.
Dress	favourit	e celebrity.
Whose	Flip me	over.

'We can sort of guess what most of the message might be – it's a birthday party, somewhere in Marrang,' Maddy mused.

'But what on earth does "Flip me over" mean?' said Lily.

Just at that moment, Janet stuck her head around the doorway. 'Girls! What are you up to? Your parents are asking where I've hidden you all!'

Everyone jumped in surprise. They had been so engrossed in the puzzle clues that they'd forgotten where they were!

As they scrambled to pick up their belongings, Sienna shoved all the clues into her sports bag. 'I'll keep them until next week, okay?' she asked.

Everyone agreed, but Jade delivered a parting comment as she started running towards her mum's car. 'If you lose them, Sienna, I'll flip *you* over – and leave you upside down!'

Chapter Thirteen

Two nights later, Phoebe settled blissfully into the cosy folds of the couch. Her parents were getting ready to go out. Max was playing on the computer. She had the TV all to herself and had prepared some drinks and snacks. She knew Caitlyn would be arriving soon to look after them and had chosen a movie they could watch together.

'Phoebe! I almost forgot!' Dad bustled in, dressed for dinner but still with bare feet and unbrushed hair. He picked up the DVD remote and started jabbing at the buttons and muttering in frustration. Nothing changed on the TV.

'Dad, what are you doing?'

'Australia's playing New Zealand – Diamonds versus Silver Ferns. I thought you'd want to watch the game,' he said, as he frowned at the remote, then up at the TV.

'But I've already picked a movie to watch,' said Phoebe.

'This will be much better . . . Urghh! This stupid thing never works!'

Phoebe giggled. Dad had no idea when it came to any form of technology. Once she had even seen him pick up the TV remote to answer the phone!

'Dad, that's the wrong remote,' she said.

The doorbell rang.

'Max, can you answer the door?' Dad

bellowed. But after a few moments had passed, it was obvious that even Dad's voice couldn't penetrate Max's concentration when he was playing computer games.

'I'll get it,' said Phoebe, and she went to let Caitlyn in.

Caitlyn was six years older than Phoebe, but Phoebe always felt relaxed with her. She seemed happy to watch the TV shows Phoebe and Max liked, and now that Phoebe had started playing netball, Caitlyn was always willing to give her tips and have a practice game.

'Got it!' said Dad, when Phoebe walked back into the lounge room, followed by Caitlyn.

'Hello, Caitlyn!' said Dad. 'Have a seat. The game's just started. Now Phoebe – this is the player you need to watch . . .'

Dad stood up, pointing out the Australian goalers and leaning in to check their names, which were written on the back of their uniforms. He was so enthusiastic that he kept shuffling closer and closer to the TV. Squinting to read the words, he completely blocked the screen so that Phoebe and Caitlyn couldn't see a thing! The girls grinned at each other.

'Watch the Goal Shooter, Phoebe. See the way she keeps working the ball out to the Wing Attack until she's close under the ring? Can't miss from there,' he said, watching and admiring the players.

'It would help if we could see through you!' said Caitlyn, laughing.

'Bill, we're running late,' Mum called out from the bedroom. Dad stepped back from the screen, reluctantly.

'Watch it, Phoebe,' he urged. 'You can learn a lot from these players.'

Phoebe had really wanted to watch the movie she had picked, but now the netball game was on, she had to admit that her dad knew her well. This was *way* better than any movie!

'Okay, Dad,' said Phoebe. 'Do you mind, Caitlyn?'

'No, I love watching the Diamonds play!'

Chapter Fourteen

Finally Mum and Dad left and the house was quiet.

Phoebe tried to watch the Australian goalers as Dad had suggested, but her eyes kept being drawn to the Goal Attack playing for the New Zealand Silver Ferns. Her movements were just so smooth and graceful, and she was unfazed by the constant jostling of the Australian defenders. She would shoot for goal from wherever she was standing, and it seemed that the ball glided through the goal ring every time, barely skimming the sides as it went.

The Australian Diamonds were winning the game, for which Phoebe was glad. Secretly, though, she cheered every time the New Zealand Goal Attack got the ball and scored again. She didn't want to admit it to Caitlyn, though, in case she thought Phoebe was being disloyal to Australia.

At the half-time break, Australia was leading by seven goals. Caitlyn wandered off to get herself another drink and to check on Max. Phoebe stayed in front of the TV, wanting to know the name of the goaler she'd been watching.

As they displayed a table of the goaling percentages, the commentators discussed the results. 'Maria Tutaia, of course, is in Goal Attack for New Zealand. She's a very consistent player, shooting at 95% accuracy tonight.'

Phoebe knew this meant that Maria Tutaia was getting almost every goal.

Maria Tutaia, Maria Tutaia, Phoebe repeated the name to herself. *I want to play like her!*

Caitlyn wandered back into the room and plonked her cup of tea down on the table. 'So who's your favourite player in the game?' she asked Phoebe.

Phoebe hesitated, unsure if she should admit to favouring a New Zealander. She shrugged noncommittally.

'Well,' said Caitlyn, 'I have to admit that whenever Maria Tutaia's on court, I'm cheering for her. She's awesome!'

'I know!' said Phoebe. 'She's amazing!'

When the third quarter commenced, Phoebe curled her legs up underneath her, keen to watch Maria Tutaia again.

'That shooting action,' Caitlyn murmured, as they watched Maria put another goal through the ring.

Phoebe nodded silently in agreement, not daring to look away from the screen in case she missed anything.

They continued to watch the game together, both completely absorbed. It was an exciting finish, with a clear win to New Zealand, who had come from behind.

Caitlyn turned to Phoebe. 'Want to try to shoot like Maria Tutaia?'

It was too dark to go outside and practise, so while they waited for the popcorn to pop, they stood up in front of the couch and mimicked the way Maria held her arms when she went for a goal.

Chapter Fifteen

It was time. Her moment had finally come. The mood in the stadium was electric. Everyone knew how tough this game was going to be, for both teams.

Phoebe's nerves were tingling. As she stood on court, waiting for the whistle to blow, she went through her last-minute ritual. It always helped to steady her nerves before the game. First she tightened her ponytail, then she adjusted her shoelaces – left foot first, then right – and, finally, she bounced on her toes to loosen the tension in her muscles.

The whistle went and the game exploded into action. Phoebe stood poised, ready for anything. Australia had the first centre pass and moved the ball quickly into their goal third. But Phoebe's teammates were ready for them. The New Zealand defenders put pressure on every pass. They quickly intercepted the ball and sent it down towards their team's goal circle. Seeing the turn of play, both the Australian defenders rushed back to defend Phoebe, the New Zealand Goal Shooter. She was blocked at every turn!

Just then, Maria flew into the goal circle. She took a pass from the New Zealand Wing Attack and turned to shoot for goal. But as soon as it left her hand, Phoebe knew it wouldn't make it. It was very rare for Maria to miss, but Phoebe was right. The ball rebounded high off the ring. Phoebe was determined to catch it. She paused deliberately and waited until the last possible moment, then she soared into the air and just managed to tip the ball up and out of the defender's hands. Snatching the ball for herself, Phoebe quickly popped it through for the first goal of the game.

One section of the crowd – the section where everyone was dressed in black and white – roared. 'Sil-ver Ferns! Sil-ver Ferns!'

Maria Tutaia turned to Phoebe and, with a wide smile, gave her a high five before turning back to be ready for the next centre pass. Phoebe grinned in delight at their successful start. She was buzzing with energy, but told herself to keep focused.

This time it was New Zealand's centre pass. The ball was heading their way. Phoebe, all senses alert, saw Maria head to the top of the goal circle. This left room for Phoebe to run along the baseline, where she took a high pass from the Wing Attack. When she turned, though, she realised that she wasn't close enough to the goal ring to make an easy shot.

'Here if you need!' she heard her team's Centre call from behind. Phoebe paused, unsure if she should pass it out or try for a goal.

'Go for it!' Maria said, standing ready under the goal ring for any rebounds.

That was all Phoebe needed. She swung the ball up and sent it flying towards the ring in one smooth action.

It made it! The Silver Ferns were on fire!

The Australian defenders were getting desperate. For the rest of the game, they crowded and blocked Phoebe and Maria, but it was as though they could read each other's minds – both of them knew when to pass to a space just before the other reached it, or whether to go for a goal or pass it to the other.

Finally the whistle sounded and the game was over. The New Zealand supporters cheered as loudly as they could. Phoebe and Maria had both scored with over 95% accuracy, and had won the game for the Silver Ferns!

'Phoebe!'

She could hear people in the crowd calling for her autograph.

'Phoebe! Phoebe, are you listening?'

Phoebe reluctantly turned around and saw her mother looking at her quizzically. The whole stadium immediately vanished.

'Phoebe, it's almost time to head down to the fete. Best come in and get ready now.'

Phoebe nodded, wondering if her mum had noticed anything while she had been practising in the backyard.

'Oh Phoebe – one more thing. Did you win for Australia?' Mum asked, with a little smile.

'Yeah, sure, Mum,' said Phoebe, rolling her eyes, pretending her mum was way off.

Thank goodness she doesn't know who I was really playing for!

Chapter Sixteen

The voices of the crowd, the tinny music of the rides and the flapping of the marquees drifted towards Phoebe and her family on the breeze. They were approaching the gates of the school grounds where the fete was being held. The fete was organised by the Marrang community and involved four of the local schools, including Phoebe's.

Phoebe stood for a moment at the gates, absorbing the spectacle of colour and movement and working out where she should start first. But her family were already heading off in three different directions!

'I'd better get going,' said Mum. 'I promised Marj I'd help at the second-hand-toy stall.'

'Here's some money for rides, kids,' said Dad, as he handed them each a generous amount. 'I'm supposed to be on the spinning wheel, so I'd better head off.' Dad had volunteered to be in charge of working the large spinning wheel. It had numbers around the edges and people bought tickets to guess the number it would stop at. They won a prize if their guess was correct. The organisers obviously knew that Dad's booming voice would be perfect for calling out the winning numbers!

'See ya,' Max said to Phoebe, with a wave. He had spotted Jordan and his other mates already getting soaked in a water fight. They were stalking each other from behind and between the marquees. Some of the adults nearby didn't look too pleased – they were getting wet in the crossfire!

Phoebe was left looking awkwardly around. Suddenly she was on her own and the fete didn't seem as much fun. She felt as if she was the only person there who wasn't hanging out with friends or family. She didn't want to look as if she didn't have anyone to hang out with, though, so she walked purposefully towards one of the stalls, which had handmade jewellery and ornaments on display. She used some of the money her dad had given her to buy a hand-painted wooden bangle. She had really only bought it for something to do, but when she put it on, she admired it as it hung from her wrist. It was bright and colourful, and reminded her of the cheerful bangles that Prani wore.

She turned and spotted the rides on the oval.

There was an inflatable jumping castle, the bungee tramps, and something called the Storm Twister. Phoebe bought some ride tickets from the ticket booth and then wandered over to get a closer look. People were being strapped into harnesses in a carriage that tipped and twisted and spun until everyone was screaming. It looked terrifying, but absolutely awesome!

'Hey Phoebe!'

Phoebe turned around and saw Jade and Isabella waiting a long way down the queue that snaked away from the entry gate to the Storm Twister. They were waving for her to come over. Phoebe felt her whole body relax. For the first time since arriving, she felt like she was part of the crowd. She hurried over.

'What's happening?' Jade asked her. 'Have you seen Jordan yet?'

'He's with Max. I just got here,' Phoebe replied.

'I heard you lost against Waroona yester-day,' said Jade.

'Yeah, they were all really, really tall and really, really good,' said Phoebe.

'You needed me there to help with goaling,' said Jade, smirking. 'Pity I was at a birthday party.'

Phoebe looked away and didn't answer.

'Did you see Sienna doing SingStar on stage?' said Isabella, kindly changing the subject. 'It was hilarious!'

Phoebe laughed. She could just imagine Sienna being brave enough to do that. 'There's no way I could do that,' Phoebe said quietly. 'What are the rides like?'

'I guess we're about to find out,' said Jade, smartly, 'but don't think you're going to cut into the line. You have go to the end and wait like the rest of us.'

Phoebe looked at her in shock. She turned

to Isabella to check with her but Isabella clearly wasn't going to speak up against Jade.

'Sorry,' Isabella mouthed to Phoebe.

Phoebe turned away. Embarrassed, she headed with eyes down towards the end of the line. It was so long that it had begun to curve and turn back on itself. Phoebe stepped in behind a group of three young boys at the end.

Is the ride even going to be worth it? she thought. *I look so stupid standing here by myself. Maybe I should just help Mum at the toy stall . . .*

Chapter Seventeen

'Phoebe! Phoebe!'

Phoebe turned at the sound of her name. Lily was calling to her from near the front of the line to the Storm Twister. Prani and Sienna were just ahead of her. Prani was waving her arms, her bangles clinking musically together.

It was nice to hear Lily's friendly voice. Phoebe stood and waved to Lily, Prani and Sienna but didn't move towards them. She wouldn't make that mistake again.

'Come over here!' Lily called to her. 'You can jump in with us!'

Sienna gave Phoebe a broad smile and stepped back, making room for her. 'You're just in time. We're about to go on.'

Should I go over to them? wondered Phoebe. *I want to . . . And they all seem a lot nicer than Jade.*

Hesitating for a moment longer, Phoebe took a deep, shaky breath, then started to move towards her teammates. When she got there, Prani started jumping around on the spot, swinging her head at weird angles.

'Prani, what are you doing?' Sienna asked.

'I'm getting ready for the ride, but it's making me feel a little dizzy!' she said, giggling and stumbling slightly.

'We're on!' Lily announced, and the four of them leapt through the gates and raced to claim a four-seat booth.

Phoebe fastened her harness, her heart thumping. The ride started and as the spinning got faster and faster, she felt the skin tighten on her face. She held on tightly. There was no space for talk. Phoebe felt as if she had to use all her concentration just to hold on! When the carriage began to jerk and change direction, she opened her mouth and, along with the other girls, screamed continuously in both fear and exhilaration.

When the ride finally came to a stop, Phoebe's legs were trembling. She stumbled along with the others out onto the oval.

Prani looked a little stunned. 'Well, my head-swinging didn't get me ready for *that*!' she said.

The others looked at her and burst out laughing.

'Hot chips?' she suggested, and they headed off to the hot-chips stand.

As they walked past the marquees, Phoebe heard Lily squeal in surprise. At the very same time, she felt a blast of cold hit her right in the middle of her back.

'Ahhh!'

She turned to see what was happening and spotted Max, Jordan and two of their mates peering around a marquee holding water pistols. All four girls stood still, the backs of their clothes dripping.

Sienna gathered herself first. 'Quick. Run!'

She sprinted towards the safety of the school hall, followed by Lily, Prani and Phoebe. The boys were in hot pursuit but the girls made it, landing, gasping, inside the doors just in time.

'Nuuumber eighty-six! Eighty-six! Does anyone have lucky number eighty-six?' Phoebe's dad's voice boomed through the microphone. He was standing right next to the girls, calling out the winning numbers on the spinning wheel.

'Phoebe!' said Dad. 'Just the girl I need! Can you help me collect money for the tickets? There are more people here than I thought there would be.'

'But Dad!' said Phoebe. She had only just started having fun with the other girls!

Dad raised his eyebrows. 'Phoebe. This is for a good cause.'

Phoebe was conscious of the girls watching. Her face flushed red. 'Okay.' She sighed and dutifully took the money tin from her dad, then turned to watch the girls moving away. With a quick wave, they bounced off through the hall.

Phoebe attempted a smile at her dad. He didn't mean to stop her making friends . . . But this was the first time she had hung out with Sienna, Prani and Lily. Would she get another chance? Would they even bother to include her next time?

Chapter Eighteen

Phoebe grabbed the mail from the letterbox as she came in through the front gate. She didn't look at the bundle of letters. She was too caught up in thoughts about training that night. She had seen dark clouds looming overhead on her walk home from the bus stop. It wasn't raining at the moment and she didn't know if she wanted it to start or not. She wanted to see her teammates again, but she didn't think she could bear going to training and listening to the others talk about the fete. She didn't want to feel left out again.

She tossed the letters onto the kitchen bench. One square white envelope slipped away from the pile of bills. Phoebe stared at it. It was addressed to her! Holding her breath in hope, she ripped it open. The familiar riddle fell out into her hand. Phoebe knew every word by heart, but she still read it with pleasure because this one was meant for her.

'Here is a puzzle to be solved by you,
when you are all down at the court.
Look out for a clue, or maybe two;
don't rush, give it plenty of thought!'

She looked back into the envelope and saw the puzzle piece sitting snugly in the corner, waiting for her.

'Mum! *Mum!* I got one!' Phoebe was so excited she couldn't contain herself. Her heart was racing and when she spotted her mum in the backyard, she rushed out to tell her the news.

'Mum, I got a clue!' she said breathlessly.

'Oh Phoebe, that's fantastic!'

Now Phoebe couldn't *wait* to get to training! *Please, rain, don't start now!* she thought.

But as soon as Phoebe and Mum got into the car, big, fat raindrops started landing on the windscreen.

'This doesn't look too promising,' Mum said, peering up at the sky.

Phoebe said nothing. She couldn't imagine Janet cancelling training for a few drops.

But as they drove, the spattering of the rain-drops became heavier and more constant, and by the time they arrived at the courts, the rain was pelting down and the wind-screen was awash. Phoebe could just make out the figures of Janet and Lily as they threw the training equipment back into their car, before jumping in themselves. There was no one else at the drenched courts. All Phoebe could see were the headlights of the other cars in the carpark, as they swung out and headed back home.

Phoebe looked out of the car window.

'Disappointed?' her mum asked kindly.

Phoebe said nothing. Then a moment later she blurted out, 'It's not fair. We were going to look at the clues together . . .'

'Don't worry. Your game is only three days away. You can show the others your clue then,' said Mum.

Yes, thought Phoebe, *the game isn't far away. I can wait until then.*

And then she smiled to herself again with the realisation that she hadn't been forgotten.

I got a clue!

Chapter Nineteen

'What's this?' Phoebe's dad asked, as her mum placed two thermoses and a tall stack of cups on the kitchen table.

'Some hot chocolate for the girls. Have you noticed how cold that wind can be when it blows onto the courts, up off the river?'

Phoebe's dad hadn't noticed, but of course he was always in a constant state of motion.

'Yum! Thanks, Mum,' said Phoebe. 'The girls will love it.'

'I thought it would be good timing, since you're taking your turn as team captain this week.'

Phoebe beamed at Mum. The prospect of being team captain had sat in her mind since Thursday night when Janet had called to tell her, and every time she had thought about it since then, she'd glowed with excitement.

'Well, let's get going then,' said Dad.

Phoebe grabbed her drink bottle and the precious clue. Mum gathered the hot chocolate and cups. Dad spent the next five minutes searching for the car keys. Then, just as they had all stepped out the door, Max realised that he was missing one of his soccer boots.

Finally they arrived at the courts. Phoebe hurried over to fill out the scoresheet. It was her first job as team captain. She checked with Janet where everyone was playing. When she listed herself as the Goal Attack, as Janet had told her to, she put a little smiley face in the 'o' of 'Phoebe'. Goal Attack! She was going to be playing in the same position as Maria Tutaia! She visualised Maria playing. She thought about Maria's fast but smooth movement down the court, and her . . .

Phoebe's thoughts were interrupted by the umpire, who appeared before her holding a coin in the palm of her hand. Phoebe's other job as team captain was to join the umpires and the opposition captain for the coin toss. The winner would get to decide whether they would choose their team's goal end, or whether to start with the ball. Phoebe proudly walked out onto the court with the umpire and smiled briefly at the small, red-haired Thomson team captain who joined them.

The Marrang Gems were the first-named team on the scoresheet, so Phoebe got to call the toss.

'Tails,' she called as the coin spun in the air. The umpire caught it and flipped it onto the back of her hand. It was tails!

'We'll take first centre pass,' said Phoebe, without hesitation. It was a still and overcast day and she knew it would be much the same goaling from either end of the court.

Phoebe joined her team.

Lily looked at her curiously. 'So who gets first centre pass?'

'We do!' said Phoebe, her eyes twinkling, 'and I've got a new clue for after the game!'

'Me too!' squealed Prani.

'Yay!' cried the team, and they turned and ran onto the court.

Phoebe felt good in her Goal Attack bib. As the first quarter wore on, she better understood her role. She knew she had to help bring the ball down the court, as well as help the Goal Shooter shoot goals.

Thomson had the next centre pass. Before their Goal Attack could catch the ball, Isabella in Goal Defence had leapt in front and snatched it out of the air. She quickly flicked it to Sienna in Wing Defence, who passed it straight on to Lily as Wing Attack. Phoebe readied herself for action, but was distracted when she sensed a flurry of activity on the sidelines of the court. She spun around to see what was happening. It was her dad! In his eagerness to follow the game, he was hurrying along the sidelines, calling out his encouragement to the players. The only problem was that he was getting in the way of the umpire!

Phoebe gestured to her dad to step back, and he looked around in surprise. He hadn't even noticed he was blocking the umpire! He stumbled backwards in haste. Phoebe glanced at Mum and Max, who were sitting on the bench by the court, smiling and shaking their heads, then winced as she saw the cross face of the umpire.

But the game was continuing, so she turned her attention to the court. Bit by bit, she began to settle back into the rhythm of the game. Maddy stepped into the centre circle, clasping the ball firmly in both hands. She nodded her head once at Lily, who nodded back. Lily was holding firm on the line, against the jostling of the Wing Defence. When the whistle sounded, Maddy ignored her Thomson Centre opponent, who waved her arms, hoping to deflect a pass. When Lily made a straight lead towards her, Maddy snapped her a quick pass and raced down court, to the edge of the goal circle.

Maddy called to Lily for the ball, then shouted out to Phoebe to prepare for the next catch. 'Go Phoebe!' she yelled.

Phoebe was ready. She sprang into action, sprinting towards the goal circle. She ran so fast that her Goal Defence opponent couldn't keep up with her! Jade, their Goal Shooter, was at the top of the goal circle, and she stood firmly against the Goal Keeper. Phoebe raced past her, glancing up just in time to catch the flying lob from Maddy.

Phoebe landed firmly on both feet, close to the goal ring, the ball in her hands. She took a precious second to correct her body position, then, raising her arms high above her head, she balanced the ball just like she'd seen Maria Tutaia do. Phoebe had no time to aim carefully at the goal ring. She had only one more second before the umpire called 'held ball'. She flicked the ball up at the ring.

It was a goal!

'Woohoo!'

'Yay Phoebe!'

Phoebe grinned as she heard the cheers of her dad, her coach and her team.

Chapter Twenty

Just after quarter time, the pace of the game increased. The Thomson netball team had swapped some of their players. It may have been because the new players were more skilled than those in the first quarter, or just because the team was settling into the game, but slowly the goals started to level.

The Thomson spectators, sensing the change in tempo on court, began to cheer more loudly. Phoebe's dad couldn't resist the opportunity to support his daughter and her team. He ran up and down along the sideline, yelling and cheering them on. Once again, Phoebe didn't know where to look – at the ball or at him.

Taking a sneaking glance at her dad, Phoebe saw him veer quickly to the left to avoid running into the umpire. He tripped over a sports bag in his path and pitched forward into a spectacular double somersault. He squashed three bags on landing and finally ended up flat on his back, staring up into the umpire's glaring face.

'*Brrrp*,' went the umpire's whistle. 'Injury time . . . for the spectator!'

'I'm okay, nothing to worry about here,' said Dad, as he struggled to his feet.

Phoebe went bright red with embarrassment. She couldn't look at any of her teammates or her coach. She was pretty sure this

was the first time in history that injury time had been called for a spectator! She stared at her dad, stunned, and watched as her mum went to help him limp over to the first-aid room.

Janet called the girls in for a team huddle.

'Okay, minor distraction everyone. Now, we need to focus for the rest of the game. Thomson is a very good team and it's going to take a lot of hard work to beat them!'

'Minor? That was the biggest crash I've ever seen!' said Jade, laughing.

Phoebe cringed at the sound of the others laughing along with her.

After a pause, though, Jade added, 'Shame he had to go. He's the best cheer squad ever!'

Phoebe looked up in surprise. She had not expected that from Jade. To her relief, she could see everyone else agree.

'Yeah, he's awesome,' said Maddy.

'Okay, Phoebe?' Janet asked. 'If you can concentrate, I'll leave you as Goal Attack for the second half as well.'

'Thanks, Janet,' said Phoebe, nodding uncertainly.

Lily appeared beside her and smiled. 'Relax, Phoebe, you're so good at shooting.'

Phoebe smiled gratefully, and when the whistle went for play to resume, she allowed herself to get drawn back into the game. Soon, all she was thinking about was getting ready for the next pass, looking for the next free player, and shooting her next goal.

She didn't even see her dad returning to sit on the bench after half-time. Mum poured him a generous serve of hot chocolate. His elbow and knee were bandaged, but he still managed to call out encouragements from time to time. Phoebe didn't really hear. She was determined to show Janet just how well she could play in

Goal Attack. In her determination, she found herself in a place where everything outside the court was zoned out and for once she was able to play her best netball.

And she needed every bit of concentration she had. Both teams were straining to get in front of the other. By the final quarter, it was turning into a battle for the Marrang Gems to keep up with Thomson, a tough team that was used to winning.

Chapter Twenty-one

There was only one minute until the end of the game and the score was tied! The time-keeper stared fixedly at the timer, watching the final seconds pass. Maddy grabbed the ball and raced into the centre circle. She nodded at Phoebe, her signal to make a lead.

The whistle blew to start play. Phoebe burst forward and caught a fast low pass from Maddy. Turning, she ignored the teammates close to her, who were calling loudly for a pass – she had seen Jade waving at her from right under the goal post.

Can I throw that far? Will it work?

Making a split-second decision, Phoebe lifted her arms high. Using her shoulder muscles, she threw the ball as hard as she could, straight and fast all the way to the goal circle. Jade saw the ball bulleting towards her. She braced her feet, and the ball smacked into her hands.

The timekeeper was standing, ready to call time to the umpires . . . Jade turned to face the goal ring and confidently popped the ball through the ring.

'Time!' called the timekeeper. *Brrrp* went the umpire's whistle.

The Marrang players looked around at Janet, unsure which team had won the game. Then they saw her grinning and holding one finger in the air. The Marrang Gems had won by one goal!

Phoebe was totally pumped with the way she had played. It felt like it had been her best game yet.

As the team came off court, they buzzed with excitement. Charlotte, who had sat out the last half of the game, came from the bench to join the girls.

'Oh my God! That last quarter was so exciting! I didn't know who was going to win!'

Phoebe smiled at Charlotte. *It* was *pretty great!* she thought, as she watched her team-mates all eagerly reaching for the hot chocolate her mum was handing out.

But the excitement of the day wasn't over. Phoebe and Prani still hadn't shown their clues to the others! Even though Phoebe knew what her clue said, she wasn't sure how it would fit into the puzzle. But she knew this much – they were very close to solving the mystery invitation.

Prani started to jump up and down on the spot. She waved her arms wildly at the group. 'Come *ooon*! Hurry up so we can put all the clues together and work out what the message says!'

She turned and ran madly towards the grass area behind the clubrooms and the rest of the team took off after her. They collapsed on the grass and looked at Sienna expectantly.

'Oh no, I forgot to bring the clues!' she said.

A chorus of horrified responses yelled at once.

'What?'

'No way!'

'You didn't!'

Sienna grinned. 'Only joking. Here they are!'

She placed the six clues they all knew on the grass in the middle of the circle and carefully arranged them in the order they had agreed upon.

Prani stretched over on her knees with her square of paper fluttering in her hand. 'Me first! Check this out!'

She tried to neatly fit her piece of the puzzle in with the others but accidently collapsed on top of the clues, spreading the pieces everywhere. She couldn't move at first because she was laughing so hard and trying to apologise at the same time.

'Prani!!'

'S-S-Sorry!'

Many hands tried to help gather the pieces – including the piece they thought they'd lost, but they found clinging to Prani's elbow. When they all settled again, they read the words on her clue:

```
┌─────────────┐
│             │
│  are invit  │
│  day p      │
│  y 15 A     │
│             │
└─────────────┘
```

'Come on, Phoebe,' Maddy urged. 'Put your piece down.'

Phoebe fit the last piece into the puzzle.

```
┌─────────────┐
│             │
│    Jump     │
│  as your    │
│   party?    │
│             │
└─────────────┘
```

'Oh my gosh!' screamed Prani. 'We're going to Jump! You know, the trampoline park!' She started bouncing on her knees. 'We're going to Jump! We're going to Jump!' she chanted.

Isabella, Maddy and Sienna joined in, and Jade clapped along. Lily and Charlotte started cheering. 'Yay! Woohoo! I can't *wait*!'

Chapter Twenty-two

Phoebe was as excited as the other girls. It was just becoming real to her that she had actually been invited to a party with her teammates! The whole invitation was clearly written for them all to see.

You birth Sunda	are invit day p y 15 A	ed to arty ugust at	a on 2.00 pm
at Dress Whose	Jump as your party?	M favourit Flip me	arrang. e celebrity. over.

Maddy asked the question they were all thinking. 'This is going to be awesome! But whose party is it?'

Everyone stared at the invitation. Phoebe murmured to herself. 'Flip me over . . . Flip me over . . .' Suddenly, she remembered there was something on the back of each of the puzzle pieces. They'd forgotten the other part of the mystery! Carefully, Phoebe began to flip over the pieces. The other girls immediately caught on and, within seconds, a photo of someone had emerged from the different scraps of colour.

As one, they looked up. Eyes wide in shock, they stared at one girl in particular.

'*Sienna?*'

Sienna grinned back, delighted. Her plan had worked perfectly! No one had suspected her at all!

'Oh my God!'

'What . . .?'

'How . . .?'

'But you got a clue as well!'

Prani threw herself at Sienna, collapsing on top of her. 'You sneaky, sneaky thing!'

Phoebe grinned at Sienna's laughing face.

'Hang on! You told me . . .' began Lily. She pointed her finger at Sienna, pretending to frown. 'I asked you at school about your birthday and you said you weren't having a party!'

Sienna shrugged casually. 'I lied.'

The girls shrieked and laughed and jumped on Sienna. It took them a long time to settle down. They lay sprawled on the grass, all eight of them thinking about what outfit they'd wear to look like their favourite celebrity.

Phoebe was in awe. 'I can't believe I got invited!'

A second later, she realised that she had accidentally spoken aloud! She glanced around in panic.

Lily, who had been lying next to her, sat up. 'Of course you would be invited. You're our netball mate! Oh, and by the way,' Lily continued, 'will you *pleeease* invite me over so we can try out your backyard mini-court together? And then you can come over to my place next!'

Phoebe stared at Lily. She felt the hugest smile spread across her face.

I'm going to a party. I have a new friend. And I'm not so shy anymore!

The Marrang Gems

Maddy Browne
Isabella Contesotto
Sienna Handley
Jade Mathison
Prani Patel
Lily Scott
Charlotte Stevens
Phoebe Tadic

Player Profile

Phoebe Tadic

Full name: Phoebe Ana Tadic
Nicknames: Phoebs, Zlata ('zlata' means 'golden girl' in Croatian)
Age: 12
Height: 152 centimetres
Family: Mum, Dad and 14-year-old brother, Max
School: Shady Gums College

Hobbies: Phoebe feels like the luckiest girl in the world because she has her very own mini netball court in her backyard! In her free time, Phoebe loves practising her netball skills, especially her goaling. Her favourite people to practise with are her dad; her babysitter, Caitlyn; and her new friend, Lily, who also plays for the Marrang Gems. Phoebe often finds herself daydreaming about being a superstar goal shooter, and although she is shy to admit it, she hopes to one day play for the New Zealand national team, the Silver Ferns. Phoebe relaxes by helping her mum make Kremšnita, her favourite Croatian dessert, which she thinks is the perfect combination of crispy, crunchy pastry and smooth, sweet custard.

Netball club: Marrang Netball Club

Netball team: Marrang Gems, the Marrang Netball Club Under 13s team

Netball coach: Janet

Training day: Wednesday

Netball uniform: Royal blue netball dress with white side panels where 'Marrang' is written in pink. Phoebe likes to wear her long hair in a plait so that it doesn't whip around in the wind and distract her when she plays.

Favourite netball positions: Goal Shooter, Goal Attack

Netball idol: Silver Ferns and Northern Mystics player Maria Tutaia

Best netball moment: Captaining the Gems and throwing a crucial pass which led to the winning goal in the final seconds of their match against the tough Thomson netball team.

Netball ambition: To become a professional netballer and shoot at 100% accuracy for a whole season.

Netball Drills

Balance Practice

1. Gather a set of cones, or any kind of marker.
2. Arrange them on the ground in a straight line so that they are 30 centimetres apart.
3. Start at one end of the line. Make your way to the other end by darting in a zigzag motion around each cone.
4. When you get to the end of the line, do the same on the way back.

HOT TIP
Plant your outside foot on the ground as you dodge. It will keep you balanced.

Be a Stunning Shooter

1. Grab a netball.
2. Stand in front of the goal post and shoot for a goal.
3. If you get the ball through the ring, take one step backwards to increase the challenge, and try shooting again.
4. If you miss, take one step forward so it will be a little easier, and try shooting again.
5. You can increase the challenge even more by stepping backwards and to the side when you get the ball through the ring.

HOT TIP
Count how many goals you get. Keep trying to beat your own score.

Be a Smart Dodger: Leading Out

1. You'll need three people for this drill, as well as a netball.
2. Choose a partner and decide who will be the attacker and who will be the defender. The third person will be holding the ball, ready to pass to the attacker.
3. Draw a line on the ground with some chalk or, if you're at the netball courts, pick one of the transverse lines.
4. The attacker and the defender stand behind the line. The person holding the ball stands in front of the line.
5. When everyone is ready, the person holding the ball calls out for the attacker to run forward. The attacker runs out as fast as they can (this is called 'leading out'), running out wide to the side (either left or right).

6. The attacker quickly changes direction, and runs the other way to take the pass.

7. While the attacker is running, the defender tries to stop the attacker from getting the ball.

8. Swap roles so all three of you can have a go at attacking, defending and passing the ball.

HOT TIP

Change direction really quickly so your defender can't keep up with you!

Netball Positions

Position	Full title	Where the player can go	Player's role
WA	Wing Attack	Centre third, your team's goal third but not the goal circle.	To deliver the ball to the GA or GS.
GA	Goal Attack	Centre third, your team's goal third and the goal circle.	To score goals and to help the GS score goals.
GS	Goal Shooter	Your team's goal third and the goal circle.	To score goals and to help the GA score goals.
C	Centre	Everywhere but the goal circles.	To deliver the centre pass. Plays an important role in both attacking and defending down the court.
WD	Wing Defence	Centre third, opposition's goal third but not the goal circle.	To prevent the opposition's WA from getting the ball and to stop them passing it to the GA or GS.
GD	Goal Defence	Centre third, opposition's goal third and the goal circle.	To prevent the opposition's GA from getting the ball and to stop them from scoring a goal.
GK	Goal Keeper	Opposition's goal third and the goal circle.	To prevent the opposition's GS from getting the ball and to stop them from scoring a goal.

Missed out on Maddy's story, the first book in the Netball Gems series? Read on for an exciting extract of Hooked on Netball

Maddy's heart began to pound as she looked up to scan the carpark. She felt her thick brown ponytail swing as she moved her head.

Where is Prani?

Prani was Maddy's best friend and she'd said she would be at training. But training was about to start and Prani wasn't anywhere to be seen. Maddy began chewing on her bottom lip and fiddling with the soft frayed hem of her navy sports shorts.

Come on, Prani! Where are you? I'm going to be the only one without a partner!

'Passing drills! Let's get started!' said Janet, the coach, as she walked briskly up and down between the pairs of girls like a sergeant major.

She was tall and wore her long dark curly hair in a messy bun.

The rest of the team began to spread out on the court and prepared to throw chest passes, but Maddy remained where she stood, clutching a ball against her stomach.

Maybe one of the others will pair with me? thought Maddy.

She looked hopefully to her friends from school, Lily and Sienna, but they had already teamed up and made a pair. Maddy eyed the other girls in her team. Training had only begun a few weeks ago so she didn't really know them very well yet. Phoebe always seemed distracted and Maddy had no idea what she was like. Charlotte seemed quiet. Isabella seemed easygoing. Jade seemed bossy and sometimes just not very nice. In the first training session she'd made some comment about Prani being Indian, which Maddy didn't get. What did it matter?

Now what? Maybe I should go and ask to be a third person for the passing drills . . . But I don't want to be annoying . . .

Maddy's mind raced.

What if the coach takes pity on me, the left-over girl, and asks me to do the passes with her? That would be the worst . . . Come on, Prani!

The seconds stretched on and for a moment, Maddy wondered why she'd even joined the Marrang Netball Club Under 13s team. Although they were officially known by their club name at games, it had been Maddy's idea to choose a special name for their team. They had chosen the Gems after the Australian team, the Diamonds.

Janet aimed a questioning look at Maddy but just as she opened her mouth to speak, a car with a broken muffler weaved noisily along the track between the gum trees, towards the carpark.

Prani leapt from the car and ran towards the courts, waving madly at Maddy. Her thick black braid bounced, and her earrings glittered in the late-afternoon sun.

'Sorry I'm late –' she began.

'Quick!' interrupted Maddy. 'We have to start or we'll miss practising chest passes!'

They found space on the court and stood about two metres apart. As they began their chest passes, they heard the coach's clear voice.

'Now remember, everyone,' Janet called, 'when you catch a chest pass, you grab it with both hands, one on either side of the ball. I want you to grab it strongly and hold tight, like a two-year-old who grabs and says "Mine!".'

Instantly, four pairs of girls began imitating a two-year-old with every catch. 'Mine! Mine! Mine! Mine!'

Maddy realised that the idea had worked. She was more conscious of pulling the ball strongly and decisively towards her each time she caught it.

Relaxed now that Prani was here, Maddy began to enjoy training. They moved from chest passes to bounce passes. It reminded her of the NetSetGO training she'd done when she was younger. NetSetGO was how she'd learnt the basic skills and rules of netball.

The trick to these kind of passes was to figure out where the ball needed to bounce so that it could be neatly caught by your partner, in front of her body. You also had to work out how much force to put behind your pass. If the pass was too strong, it would bounce too high. If it was too soft, it would bounce too low, making it difficult to catch.

Prani used the right amount of force but her aim wasn't that great because she was distracted, telling Maddy all about why she was late. Maddy lunged sideways to catch Prani's crooked pass.

'So anyway,' Prani continued, 'Nani wanted to start teaching me how to cook, but Mum said she had to wait until after netball training. They talked on and on and on and *on* about it – and *that's* why I'm late!'

Maddy laughed. Prani often talked about her funny grandma, who she called 'Nani'.

The team shifted to practising lob passes. Maddy stepped forward on her left foot and carefully lobbed the ball just high enough for Prani to do a standing leap and stretch her arms high to catch the pass. Maddy's quick, sharp passes contrasted with Prani's loose, fluid movements. Maddy relished the feel of the new netball in her hands. Now she'd be ready for any type of pass in Saturday's game!

Maddy

NETBALL GEMS
netball

Hooked on Netball

B.HELLARD and L.GIBBS

Phoebe

NETBALL GEMS
netball

Chase Your Goal

B.HELLARD and L.GIBBS

Lily

NETBALL GEMS
netball

Pivot and Win

B.HELLARD and L.GIBBS

Maia

NETBALL GEMS
netball

Defend to the End

B.HELLARD and L.GIBBS

Jade

NETBALL GEMS
netball

Aim for the Top

A.DARLISON

Sienna

NETBALL GEMS
netball

Keeping it Real

A.DARLISON

Prani

NETBALL GEMS
netball

Go with the Flow

B.HELLARD and L.GIBBS

Sakur

NETBALL GEMS
netball

Count Me In

B.HELLARD and L.GIBBS

COLLECT THE SERIES